For Pat Jackson, a unicorn friend—P. B.
For Joy, with gratitude—M. G.

Text copyright © 1992 by Margaret Greaves
Illustrations copyright © 1992 by Pauline Baynes

First published 1992 by J.M. Dent & Sons Ltd
First U.S. edition 1993

Library of Congress Cataloging-in-Publication Data
Greaves, Margaret.
The naming/by Margaret Greaves; illustrated by Pauline Baynes.
p.   cm.
"Gulliver books."
Summary: In the very beginning of things, before time itself, Adam
names all the animals, finishing with the secret and beautiful
unicorn.
ISBN 0-15-200534-X
[1. Animals—Names—Fiction. 2. Unicorns—Fiction.]
I. Baynes, Pauline, ill. II. Title.
PZ7.G8Nam   1993
[E]—dc20   91-24144

The illustrations for this book were prepared using gouache and ·
colored pencils.

Printed in Italy

A B C D E

HBJ

Margaret Greaves

The Naming

Illustrated by Pauline Baynes

Gulliver Books

Harcourt Brace Jovanovich, Publishers

San Diego   New York   London

In the very beginning of things, before time itself began, all the creatures of the world came to Adam to learn their names. By their names the animals came to know themselves, for names have great power.

"You are Lion," Adam said to the first creatures.

"What is Lion?" asked the great beasts.

"Lion is splendor, Lion is strength, Lion is courage, Lion is danger."

"Go, and be blessed."

The lions lashed their tails joyfully, roared,
and padded off into the jungle.

Two small creatures hopped close to Adam's feet.

"You are Rabbit," he told them.

"What is Rabbit?"

"Rabbit is furriness, Rabbit is the joy of spring mornings, Rabbit is shyness, Rabbit can read the wind."

"Go, and be blessed."

The rabbits wrinkled their noses and
twitched their long ears and hopped away
into the grass.

Two slender, great-eyed, delicate-footed
creatures came before Adam.
  "You are Deer," he said.
  "What is Deer?"
  "Deer is horned beauty, Deer is speed,
Deer is timidity."

"Go, and be blessed."

With a flick of their white rumps, the deer
flashed off into the dappled shadows.

Two pairs of steady brown eyes looked up hopefully.

"You are Dog," Adam said to them.

"What is Dog?"

"Dog is loyalty, Dog is intelligence, Dog is protection and sometimes danger."

"Go, and be blessed."

But the dogs sighed contentedly and lay down
beside Adam, their heads on their paws.

Two small black specks appeared on Adam's right foot.

"You are Flea," he said to them.

"What is Flea?"

"Flea is the leaper, Flea is vexation, Flea keeps humankind in its place, showing that God makes things for their own sake and not for human convenience.

"Go, and be blessed."

The fleas giggled, though no one could hear
them, and hopped onto the dogs — leaving
two small red marks on Adam's foot.

Finally, all the creatures of the earth were
named.

All but one . . .

Last of all, this one approached timidly. Tears
shone in its beautiful eyes.

"Lord Adam, what of me?"

"I have a horn, but I am not Deer. I have strength, but I am not Lion. I have hooves and speed and fire in my heart, but I am not Horse."

"All other creatures have mates, but there is only one of me. What am I?"

The creature's milk-white hide and shining
mane glittered like a fall of stars. Adam
stroked the arch of its neck lovingly.

"You are not like the rest. They will live a
length of time, have children, and die. But
you will live always. You are the secret beauty
that haunts all dreams. You will be sought
and glimpsed but never captured. You will
remind men and women of the glory and the
mystery of life. You need no mate. Be happy
in your beauty and your freedom."

"Go, and be blessed. You are UNICORN."

The unicorn snorted with delight and whirled away like a meteor into the depths of the forest, and the stars in the heavens sang for joy.